For FRED, C.M.
For ANNE, H.R.

Many thanks to the staff and children at
Chalvey Nursery School and Assessment Unit,
and Salt Hill Nursery, Slough, Berkshire
for their help and advice.

Copyright © 2000 Zero to Ten Limited
Text copyright © 1996 Hannah Reidy
Illustrations copyright © 1996 Clare Mackie

Publisher: Anna McQuinn, Art Director: Tim Foster
Art Editor: Sarah Godwin, Designer: Suzy McGrath

First published in Great Britain in hardback in 1996
This edition published in 2000 by Zero to Ten Limited
327 High Street, Slough, Berkshire, SL1 1TX

A CIP catalogue record for this book is available from the British Library.

ISBN 1-84089-071-1
Printed in Hong Kong

Crazy Creature
Capers

Written by
Hannah Reidy

Illustrated by
Clare Mackie

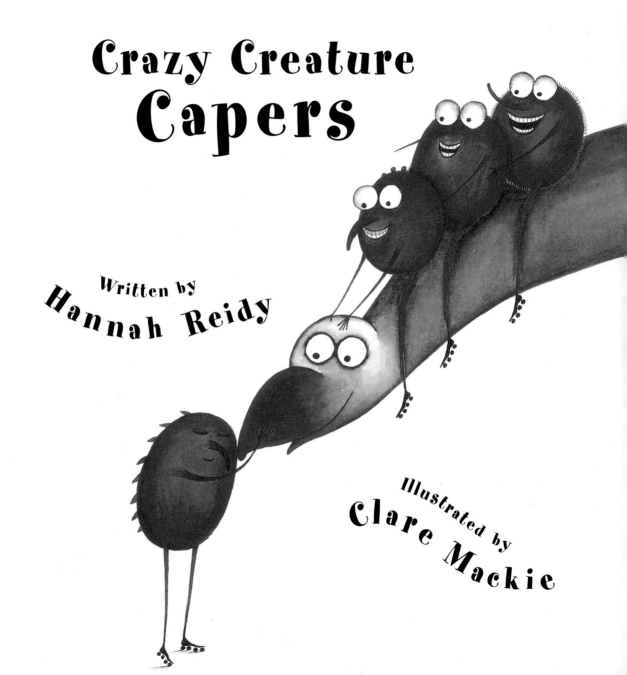

The crazy creatures put on their skates...

and

whizz

down

the

road.

To the party.

They
swoosh
under
the
crazy
bridge...

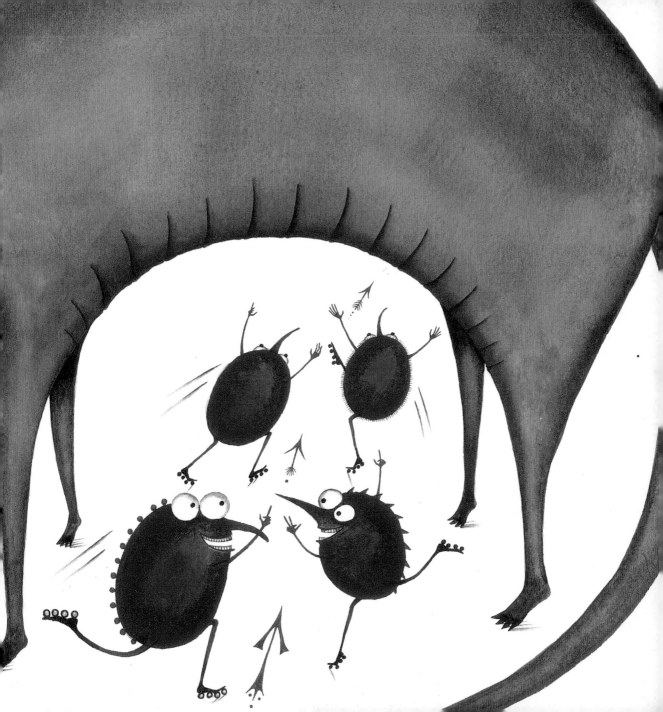

and
glide
between
the
crazy
trees.

They puff and puff and puff **up** the crazy hill...

and

tumble

over

the

knobbly

bumps.

They
whoosh
through
the
crazy
tunnel...

and
arrive
at
the
crazy
party!